DEVTA KUND

THE GOD'S POND:

The Village of Secrets (Season One)

By Sujeet N Mishra

Copyright Page

DEVTA KUND

The God's Pond: The Village of Secrets (Season One)

by **Sujeet N. Mishra**

ISBN: 978-93-344-4997-6

First Edition: 2025

Cover Design: Sujeet N. Mishra

Interior Formatting: Sujeet N. Mishra

---

9 789334 449976

Disclaimer

This book is a work of fiction.

Names, characters, places, and incidents

Publisher's Note

This edition of *Devta Kund: The God's Pond — The Village of Secrets (Season*

TABLE OF CONTENTS

Prologue

The Pond That Remembers

There are stories that live longer than the people who tell them.

In the heart of the mountains, where the pines grow so densely that the sky disappears between their arms, there lies a village that has learned to forget. Its lanes are narrow, its rooftops old, and its people speak softly, as if every word must be measured before the mountains decide whether to keep it or echo it back.

Just beyond the last house, beyond the terraced fields and the hushed grazing grounds, lies Devta Kund—a pond so still that it never ripples, not even when the wind sighs through the valley. It lies nestled in an ancient hollow, guarded by cliffs that lean inward like the ribs of a vast stone beast. The villagers believe the place breathes, though no one has ever said it aloud.

They do not go near it at dusk.

Not since the night of the thunderstorm.

They still speak of it, in whispers.
Not of the event itself, but of the silence that followed.

Before the storm, Devta Kund was a sacred place. A place where offerings were made and prayers were left. A place where the boundary between the living world and whatever lies beyond felt thinner — like a fabric stretched too tightly.

But that was before he disappeared.

The Man Who Heard the Water Speak

His name was Devendra Thakur, born in 1902 in the hills. Although he was raised in a village, he pursued his education in the cities, where knowledge was both vibrant and dynamic. He returned to the village not out of a belief in its traditions, but out of a desire to understand them. As a teacher, he was curious, rational, and patient; however, there was something about him that instilled fear in the village elders.He asked *why*.

Why did the pond glow under certain stars?
Why did the birds avoid the trees around it?
Why did no one throw stones into its water, not even as children?

The villagers told him the place was sacred.
Devendra heard only *secret*.

He returned night after night, notebook and lantern in hand.
He observed. He measured. He listened.

And slowly, the silence of the place began to speak back to him.

There were nights when the water shimmered though no wind blew.
Nights when shadows shifted though nothing moved.
Nights when footsteps sounded behind him though he stood alone.

But Devendra was not afraid.

He believed knowledge could not harm him.

In time, he was no longer alone at the pond.

She began to accompany him.

A young woman of the village, gentle and curious — Somnath's daughter, known for her laughter that once carried like chimes through summer orchards. People later tried to forget her name, but the mountains remember everything.

Together, they sat on the moss-covered stones and watched the water.

They spoke not of gods, not of fear, not of the villagers' warnings.

They spoke of *possibilities*.

The Night the Sky Fell into Water

Then came the monsoon night of 1943.

The air that evening was heavy, as if soaked in silence. Lightning crawled along the clouds like veins of burning silver. The villagers shut doors early. Dogs whimpered and hid beneath beds.

Devendra and the girl walked toward the pond.

Some watched them pass.
None called out.
None tried to stop them.

For in a village that remembers everything, there are moments it chooses to forget.

At midnight, a flash of lightning split the sky.

The pond glowed — not with reflection, but from within.

A pillar of cold, shimmering light rose upward from the water, silent and absolute, stretching skyward as if the earth itself had opened a window into something older than time.

And then—

Silence.

Devendra and the girl were gone.

No splash.
No struggle.
Their shoes were found neatly placed on the stone ledge.

As if they had stepped out of themselves.

The villagers never spoke of it again.
Somnath never forgave the world.
Devendra's wife wept until her body forgot how to produce tears.
The child, still too young to understand loss, would grow up carrying an absence he could never name.

A year later, the family left the village.

They changed their surname.

And the story was buried.

But stories do not die.

They lie waiting.

In bloodlines.
In dreams.
In reflections on still water.

And seventy-five years later, when the mountains grew restless again and a young man named Rohit began to see lights near Devta Kund, the villagers felt a familiar shiver pass through their bones.

The pond had awakened.
The circle had begun to open again.
The past had begun to return.

Because Devta Kund does not remember faces.

It remembers connections.

And when the past calls, time listens.

Someone always answers.

CHAPTER 1 — The Return

Timeline: Present Day — Year 2020

Location: Mumbai & Ancestral Village of Devta Kund, Northern Hills

Mumbai shimmered beneath a haze of neon and dust, a restless city that measured time in deadlines and traffic lights. Its streets pulsed with urgency, its people moved as if chased by invisible clocks, and its air vibrated with ambition.

Rohit Sharma was no different. A data analyst for a rising tech firm, he spent his days buried in numbers, algorithms, and presentations that decided other people's futures. From his twelfth-floor apartment, he could see the city stretching endlessly, each tower glittering like a circuit in some vast machine. Once, that view had filled him with pride. Lately, it only made him feel small.

Every morning began the same: a silent cup of coffee, a scroll through crowded emails, and the hum of engines below. His life was efficient, precise—and empty in ways he couldn't define.

He had left his hill village years ago, chasing education, opportunity, escape. The city had given him success, even love; Meera, his colleague and girlfriend, often teased that he was "married to logic." Yet something inside him had begun to stir—something that logic could not quiet.

It started with the dreams.

Each night he found himself standing beside a pond beneath a cold white moon. The water was perfectly still, reflecting the stars as if the sky had sunk into it. From across the surface came a woman's voice, soft and urgent.

"Rohit... are you here?"

And then, just before he woke, another name—his own voice this time—echoed back: "Anuja."

He told himself it was stress, the side-effect of endless work. But the dreams returned, clearer each time, until they began to feel less imagined and more remembered.

When his mother called to say his grandmother's health was failing, Rohit booked his ticket home. It was practical: convince them to move to Mumbai, closer to hospitals, away from the isolation of the hills. But beneath that reasoning lay a pull he could not explain—the same pull that had begun in his dreams.

The train pushed north through fading light. The skyscrapers gave way to fields, then to forested slopes. Rohit leaned against the window, watching the world blur into green and gold. The smell of wet soil seeped in through the gaps, awakening memories he thought he'd buried.

His phone buzzed.

Mother: *Reached? We made your favorite kheer. Your father is waiting at the station.*

A smile tugged at him. For a moment he forgot the endless reports, the city noise, the sleepless nights.

By the time the train hissed to a stop, dusk had wrapped the valley in violet fog. The small platform looked unchanged—cracked tiles, a rusted bench, a single flickering lamp. His father waited there, tall and lean, the same white kurta, a trace of chalk on one sleeve.

“Still teaching till the last day?” Rohit said, hugging him.

His father chuckled. “Old habits die hard. And besides, the children still need a teacher who stays longer than a month.”

They drove through narrow lanes where shadows hung between houses. The same banyan tree still marked the village entrance, the same milestone still leaned near the temple wall—but the voices were fewer, the windows darker.

“When we first came here, it was full of life,” his father said quietly. “Now it feels... empty.”

Rohit looked out at the sleeping fields. “Maybe everyone moved away.”

“Maybe,” his father murmured, eyes on the road. “Or maybe the place learned to keep its silence.”

Their house, recently renovated and painted, stood at the edge of the village with a red-tiled roof and clay-colored walls. Two ancient banyan trees guarded the gate like old sentries. As he returned home, his mother met him at the door, her smile bright and glistening with tears.

“Rohit! You’ve lost weight again,” she scolded, hugging him hard.

He laughed. The scent of sandalwood and cardamom filled the room, warm and familiar. Dinner was simple—lentils, rice, and his mother’s sweet kheer. They spoke for hours: city stories, old neighbors, the school. Yet under the comfort lingered something unspoken, a shadow between sentences.

As the conversation slowed, Rohit's eyes wandered across the room. Family photographs lined the walls—his parents, his childhood portraits—but none older than that. No framed ancestors, no garlanded pictures as most village homes kept. The absence felt deliberate.

"Where's the old family album?" he asked lightly.

His mother hesitated. "Ask your grandmother," she said.

From the corner, his grandmother's voice drifted through the half-light. "We lost most of it when the house was shifted. Nothing left worth keeping."

Rohit nodded, though something in her tone unsettled him.

The next morning, dawn broke through mist thick enough to blur the hills. The air smelled of wet pine and earth. He spent the day meeting childhood friends, listening to stories that all ended the same way—"Things aren't what they used to be." Yet whenever he mentioned his family name, Sharma, the elders paused before replying, as if tasting the word before releasing it.

Near sunset, an old shopkeeper stopped him at the market.

"You're Ramesh's boy, aren't you?"

Rohit smiled. "Yes, sir."

The man nodded slowly. "You look like him... or maybe like someone else."

"Someone else?"

The man shook his head. "Memory plays tricks when you get old. Forget I said it."

But the look in his eyes lingered—a mix of recognition and unease.

Before returning home, Rohit turned down the forest trail behind the house. The path wound between mossy stones and whispering pines until the trees opened into a clearing.

Devta Kund.

It looked exactly as in his dreams—circular, glass-still, reflecting the sky with unnatural precision. A narrow stream from the mountain fed it continuously, the small waterfall above shimmering in the last light of dusk.

Rohit knelt by the edge and touched the surface.

The water was cold—not the fresh chill of mountain springs, but steady, metallic cold, as if the pond's temperature never changed.

Ripples spread outward in perfect circles.

He pulled out his phone, opened the compass app. The needle spun wildly, refusing to find north.

“That’s odd,” he whispered.

He stood there until the stars appeared. The pond mirrored the heavens flawlessly, every constellation sharp, every detail exact—too exact. It felt less like reflection and more like a window.

When he returned home, his mother scolded him for being late. His father handed him a towel, saying nothing. But both looked at him as though they sensed something he couldn’t name.

That night, he dreamed again.

The same woman, the same pond, the same moon.

She called softly across the water.

"Devendra... why did you leave me here?"

Rohit woke with a start, his breath ragged, his skin damp with cold sweat.

The name echoed in his ears long after the night went still.

He didn't know it yet, but the dreams had followed him home.

Chapter 2 (Devta Kund) The Pond

Timeline: Present Day — Year 2020 — Day 2 in Village

Morning arrived wrapped in a silver mist drifting low across the village. From his window, Rohit watched pale sunlight sift through it, forming faint beams that reached toward the distant fields. The birds were calling, but their voices sounded muted, as if softened by the mist itself.

Breakfast was simple: poha warm from the stove, ginger tea steaming in cups, and his mother speaking softly about everyday things. His father sat with the morning newspaper open, his brows drawn slightly together.

"Dad," Rohit said, noticing a small column near the bottom of the page, "this says shepherds found dead cattle near the northern trail. Any idea what's happening?"

His father didn't look up. "Wolves, perhaps. The forest changes when people start leaving it."

The tone wasn't dismissive. It was *remembering*.

Rohit let the silence settle and asked about Dadi. His mother explained she was resting, not feeling well. Concern tugging at him, Rohit stepped into her room.

Dadi lay on her side, wrapped in a shawl.

"What happened to your health?" he asked gently.

"Nothing serious," she murmured. "Some days, the heart grows tired."

"Don't worry about anything," Rohit told her. "Rest. I'll come back to check on you after I go look around the village."

He was turning to leave when something in the corner caught his eye.

An old wooden trunk.

A name written across the top in faded ink:

Devendra.

The sight struck something deep inside him.

He had not heard that name spoken in years. Devendra Sharma — the ancestor whose name everyone avoided. At weddings, festivals, or funerals, the moment someone mentioned him, the conversation would grow quiet and dissolve.

A flash tore through his mind — the dream.

The glowing pond.

The violet sky.

A voice calling across the water.

"Devendra..."

His pulse skipped.

Why did it sound like a name he recognized from somewhere far older than memory?

"Where did you find this trunk?" Rohit asked softly.

Dadi opened her eyes.

"In our old house," she said.

Then, after a beat: "It belongs to you."

Rohit carried the trunk to his room and opened it carefully. Inside were letters gone pale with age, a rusted fountain pen, and a copper coin etched with a symbol — a circle enclosing a wave-like line.

Devta Kund ka Nishaan

The mark of the God's Pond.

His breath caught.

The dream pond.

The real pond.

He lifted the letters. Among them lay one sealed envelope, addressed not to **Devendra Sharma**, but:

Devendra Thakur

The surname difference struck him immediately.

So the family name had changed.

He had heard the rumor about his family from the villagers many times, and after hearing the same name in his dream, he felt a curiosity to know the actual truth.

However, he knew that if he asked his father, he would not get an answer. So, he decided that since he already had other work at the panchayat, he could also gather details about the confusion surrounding that surname at the panchayat office.

He walked to the Panchayat office, the air cool and damp against his skin. The old clerk pulled a brittle register from a shelf, pages yellowed and soft at the edges.

Rohit traced the name with a fingertip.

Devendra Thakur.

It felt heavier now.
Like a weight being passed down.

"What happened to him?" Rohit asked.

The clerk's eyes dimmed. "Old story. Some tragedy. Records were lost when the archives flooded."

"What kind of tragedy?" Rohit pressed.

The man hesitated.

"It's better not to ask about old things, beta. People moved on."

Then he added, as if the words had been waiting behind his teeth:

"My grandfather once said your family took the name *Sharma* after that tragedy. To start over."

The cold wind that followed him out of the office seemed to answer what no one else would say.

Back home, Rohit returned to his room and took the sealed letter into his hands. The wax was cracked but still clinging to the flap, like a memory refusing to release itself.

Before he could open it, a neighbor called him from outside. Startled, he tucked the letter under his pillow.

He told himself he would read it that night.

Afternoon light dimmed early under monsoon clouds. Something inside him — something he could neither name nor resist — pulled him back toward the forest.

Devta Kund.

He took his camera and notebook, telling his mother he was only walking. She reminded him to return before dusk; the winds were rising.

The trail wound between trees whose roots coiled like old veins. Even the rustle of leaves seemed muted, as though the forest was listening.

The clearing opened.

The pond lay still beneath a thin veil of mist, the waterfall feeding it in a silver thread. The surface was a perfect mirror — sky, trees, light — too perfect.

Rohit crouched and touched the water.

Cold. Not natural.

Cold like metal, steady and unchanging.

He opened the compass app. The needle spun uncontrollably.

He stayed until the stars emerged.

The pond reflected them with impossible clarity — no ripple, no distortion — as though another sky lived beneath the surface.

That night, he finally opened the letter.

The paper was fragile. The ink had faded but was still legible.

To Rohit Sharma,

Stay away from Samey Kund. Do not try to change the past.

The anomaly follows blood — memory — repetition.

This is no longer an experiment. The circle is closing.

— **Rohit Sharma, 1953**

His own name.

Written in handwriting identical to his.

His world stopped.

After reading the letter, Rohit changed.

He began visiting **Devta Kund** every morning, notebook in hand, and returned only after dark. Within a week, he stopped working, stopped eating with his family, and even stopped answering Meera's calls.

Each day he seemed to drift further away—his eyes distant, his thoughts locked somewhere beyond reach. At night, he sat by the window, tracing the strange symbol from **Devta kund**, whispering to himself as if the pond were listening.

The villagers said they often saw him by the water long after midnight, standing still, staring into his reflection. Some swore they saw another figure beside him.

On the 12th day, rain began to fall softly and whispering. Rohit stepped outside. Far in the forest, a faint blue glow pulsed from the direction of Devta Kund. He didn't think; he simply moved. The pond shimmered with a rhythm — three short pulses, pause, two long — deliberate. Calling.

He switched off his flashlight.

The pond brightened.

The reflection blinked — half a second late.

It was not mirroring him.

It was *observing* him.

His voice trembled.

"What are you?"

The water did not speak.

It *answered.*

A surge of visions tore through him:

A mountain.

A cave.

A woman's voice calling—

"Devendra!"

Darkness swallowed everything.

When morning came, Rohit's room was empty.

Only his wet shoes remained by the door.

And a faint trail of mud fading into silence.

Chapter 3 — The Search

Timeline: Year 2020 — Week 1 after Rohit's Return

Morning came shrouded in a fog so thick it swallowed the mountains whole. The village, which had seemed calm and warm just a day earlier, now felt distant—paused, as if time itself was hesitant to move forward.

Rohit's mother entered his room, expecting to hear the clatter of his morning routine. Instead, the bed lay untouched. His raincoat, soaked through, hung heavy near the door, and a pair of muddy shoes rested beside the porch. She dialed his number instinctively.

The phone was switched off.

“Ramesh,” she called, her voice tight, “have you seen Rohit this morning?”

Her husband stepped into the hall. “No. I’ve been here since early morning. I didn’t hear him leave.”

“He didn’t take his bag,” she whispered.

Ramesh placed a steadying hand on her shoulder. “Don’t worry. I’ll ask the neighbors.”

But by noon, worry had grown into panic.

The search began.

Anuj arrived unexpectedly that same afternoon – driving straight from Mumbai, intending to surprise Rohit. Instead, he found Rohit's mother pacing the courtyard, her eyes red with fear.

"What happened?" Anuj asked.

"He didn't come home last night," she said. "His phone is off."

Anuj tried calling anyway.
Silence.

Rohit's father approached Anuj urgently and asked, "Did Rohit mention anything to you before coming here?" Rohit had been disturbed since the day he came home and seemed tense all the time. "Did you talk to him today on the phone? Did he tell you anything about what was going on?"

"Yes," I talked to him, but not today; it was yesterday morning, Anuj said slowly. "He was... excited. He told me he'd found something interesting in the village. He mentioned that he wanted to show me a Kund, which he called... the only place that felt different."

Rohit's father's voice nearly broke.

"Did he say Devta Kund?"

"Yes," Anuj replied. "Devta Kund."

By evening, half the village was searching.

Lanterns bobbed through the forest like swaying stars.

The once-peaceful trail to Devta Kund now felt endless beneath flickering light.

When the darkness became too dense and the terrain too dangerous, the search was called off.

At dawn, police arrived. Inspector Karan Singh led the inquiry.

He studied Rohit's room carefully — the half-open drawer, the charging phone left behind, the muddy footprints fading toward the back door.

"This was not planned," Karan murmured. "He left suddenly. And he meant to come back."

Following the family and Anuj, he walked the forest trail to Devta Kund.

A faint metallic scent hung in the air around the clearing.

Karan knelt at the edge and dipped his fingers into the water.

"Cold," he said quietly. "Far colder than it should be."

A constable soon called out from the opposite bank.

"Sir. We found his phone."

Cracked. Mud-dried. Silent.

Meera Arrives

By afternoon, the news had reached the city.

Meera arrived with dust still clinging to her jeans, her eyes bloodshot from the journey and sleepless anxiety. The moment she stepped into the courtyard, she spoke — no hesitation, no greeting:

"He's not gone. I can feel him. He's still here."

The conviction was too sharp to be dismissed.

When Inspector Karan questioned her, she told him:

“He called me last night. Around nine-thirty. He said he saw something in the water. Something... alive. Then the call cut. I thought it was a bad signal.”

She paused, her voice lowering.

“He had been dreaming about the pond for weeks — dreams of a woman calling his name. Sometimes she called him Devendra. He told me the water glowed. I didn’t believe him. I thought it was stress.”

Phone records confirmed the last signal at **10:03 PM**, pinged directly at Devta Kund.

That evening, a technical survey team scanned the pond. After hours of mapping sonar readings, the team leader frowned at his display.

"There's a hollow beneath this. Not a cave — a chamber. And the readings... are rhythmic."

"Meaning?" Karan asked.

"Meaning the ground is emitting electromagnetic pulses. Regular ones."

Karan's expression hardened. "Engineered?"

"We don't know," the technician said. "But it isn't natural."

They did not find Rohit that night.

The Reflection Moves

Meera refused to leave the clearing.

She sat at the pond's edge until dusk, staring into the still surface.

"Rohit," she whispered, "if you can hear me... please show me something."

For a moment, the water stirred — though the air remained perfectly still.

Anuj froze.

"Meera... the reflection. It—moved."

She turned sharply. "What?"

He pointed. The water was still again.

Reflections normal.

"You're tired," she murmured.

But her pulse was racing.

Because she *had* seen it too.

A blink.

Not of water —

of whatever was *beneath* it.

The First Clue

Later that night, while checking Rohit's belongings, Anuj found a folded page hidden deep beneath the bedframe. A hand-drawn sketch of Devta Kund filled the page — coordinates scrawled along the edges.

Below, in hurried handwriting:

The reflection is not just an image.

It is a window.

Pinned to the page was a name:

Devendra Thakur

Meera's breath caught when she saw it.

"He was researching something. Trying to remember this name."

The next morning, Anuj and Meera visited Sharda Devi.

The old woman sat near the window, hands wrapped around a cup of tea. Her eyes shifted the moment Meera spoke:

"Dadi... do you know someone named Devendra Thakur?"

The tea rippled.

Her grip trembled.

"Where did you hear that name?" she whispered.

Meera held up the note. "It was in Rohit's room."

Silence stretched.

"I told Ramesh not to come back to this village," Sharda finally said. "We changed our name to Sharma to escape what happened. But the past follows blood. Always."

Anuj leaned forward. "What happened to Devendra?"

"He found something in the Kund," she whispered. "Something no one should. And like Rohit, he... disappeared."

Meera's voice shook. "His great-grandfather?"

Sharda nodded.

"Devendra Thakur. A scholar. A seeker. But some truths are not meant to be understood. When the world becomes the experiment, the world experiments back."

Her voice fell to a hush.

"If you dig up what was buried... it will come for you too."

That night, Meera and Anuj sat on the veranda, the village lights dimming one by one. The forest hummed softly — a low pulse, steady and mechanical.

Anuj exhaled. “If Devendra vanished the same way Rohit did... maybe what he found is still here.”

Meera stared toward the dark silhouette of the mountain.

“Then that’s where we go next.”

A cold breeze moved through the trees — rhythmic, measured, alive.

Somewhere beneath that mountain,

the past was awake.

Chapter 4 — The Edge of Reflection and The Hidden Experiment

Timeline: Year 2020 — Two Days After the Disappearance

FLASHBACK: Year 1937–1943 — British Research Annex (Project V)

Morning broke through a mist thick enough to soften every sound. Light seeped into Rohit's empty room, illuminating dust motes that danced in silvery threads across the cracked window glass. The air smelled of damp soil and the faint metallic tang that always lingered after rain — the same scent that had filled the air the night he vanished.

Meera woke with her dream still echoing in her mind — a dark pond, rippling without wind, and a pale face staring up at her from beneath the water's surface. The sensation clung to her skin like humidity, refusing to fade.

The sound of shifting paper drew her attention to the desk. Beneath a pile of weathered files lay Rohit's leather notebook, warped by moisture and darkened at the edges as if singed by time. She had not dared open it since the police returned it, but that morning, a strange compulsion took over.

She unlatched the strap. The scent of ink and old leather filled the room.

Most pages were smeared sketches and half-finished thoughts, but halfway through, the handwriting changed — sharper, urgent, almost feverish. Between hastily written lines, she found references to the British Research Division, an annex, and a project labeled only as "Project V."

Many words had faded, but several names stood clear — Devendra Thakur, listed repeatedly alongside British researchers studying *light resonance and reflection anomalies* detected in the pond's surface. One of the reports identified the Devta Kund as "Source Zero."

A knock startled her. Anuj stood in the doorway, rain still dripping from his jacket.

"They've called off the search again," he said quietly. "The flooding's too bad."

Meera handed him the notebook, open to the marked pages. He read silently, his brow furrowing.

"So this was a British facility?" he asked. "And Devendra's name is in their notes?"

"Yes," she replied. "Rohit believed the pond wasn't superstition at all — it was science, something the British tried to understand. He must've gone there for answers. If we can find the annex, maybe we can find him — and the truth about Devendra's experiments."

Anuj nodded. "I'll ask around about the old research site."

The Forgotten Path

By noon, the fog began to thin. Anuj found Prakash, a villager who knew the hills better than most.

"Old British building?" Prakash repeated, frowning. "Yes, it's there — up north, near the forest edge. Locked and abandoned. Nobody goes that way anymore. They say the British did something strange there before they left."

When Anuj relayed the information, Meera's eyes hardened with resolve.

“They kept writing about the pond,” she said. “Rohit — the rational one, the man who trusted only data — was trying to prove something. A bridge between belief and physics.”

Anuj exhaled. “Then that’s where we start. If answers exist, they’re waiting there.”

The road north had long been forgotten. Asphalt cracked open by roots and weeds. The silence deepened with every step they took. Even the wind seemed reluctant to move through this place.

After nearly an hour, they saw the iron gates rising ahead — flanked by stone pillars streaked with moss. A rusted plaque clung to one side. Anuj brushed away grime until faint letters emerged beneath his fingers:

“British Research Division — Project V — 1937.”

Meera's throat tightened. "It's real."

The chain across the gates had rusted through. They pushed it open; the hinges screamed.

Beyond stood a low, rectangular structure of grey stone. Windows shattered. Vines climbing up its walls like veins. The building breathed neglect.

"This is where they hid their work," Anuj murmured.

Inside, the air was thick with rust, dust, and age. Faded signs lined the corridors:

Optical Wing A. Containment Room. Resonance Chamber.

Inside the Annex

In the main hall, a tilted file cabinet leaned against the wall. A stencil across its front still read:

PROJECT V — REFLECTION STUDIES.

Meera pried open a drawer. Inside lay bundles of brittle pages — blurred ink, but still legible.

> *Preliminary Observations — Subject: "The God's Pond"*

> *Location Coordinates: 2 km east of Research Annex*

> *Water exhibits persistent reflection independent of light source.*

> *Recorded echo of spoken phrase sustained 3.2 seconds post-silence.*

> *Hypothesis: Surface retains cognitive imprint.*

Another sheet, stamped CONFIDENTIAL, described a chilling incident:

> *Test 12 — Exposure duration exceeded threshold. Two assistants reported seeing identical reflections. Subject entered water. Recovery incomplete. Directive: Suspend further field tests.*

Meera's voice trembled. "They were experimenting on the pond — on people."

Anuj exhaled. "When they failed, they must've built this place to recreate the same phenomenon under control."

Thunder rolled outside, echoing down the empty corridors.

A half-open door waited at the end of the hall, leading to a stairwell descending into darkness.

Above it, faded letters still read:

SUB-LEVEL ACCESS — AUTHORIZED PERSONNEL ONLY.

The Sub-Level

The stairs descended into cold air that smelled faintly metallic. The hum grew louder the deeper they went. At the bottom stretched a wide chamber supported by rusted iron beams. Circular engravings covered the concrete floor — symbols identical to the Nishaan carved into Devendra's old coin.

At the room's center stood a massive frame, its glass surface cracked and shimmering faintly — like a broken mirror that refused to die.

Anuj knelt beside a rusted control box. A loose page slipped free and fluttered across the floor. The paper bore the British insignia.

> *Phase 4 Report: Artificial replication of Source Zero achieved — 22% stability.*

> *Subject echo retained auditory signature for 72 hours post-exposure.*

> *Risk of cross-imprint transfer confirmed. Recommend termination.*

"Transfer," Anuj muttered, reading aloud. "As if something passes between the real and reflected."

Before Meera could respond, the air vibrated — a faint hum trembling beneath their feet. The mirror-frame pulsed once with dim light, like a heartbeat long forgotten.

"The British didn't fail," Anuj said quietly. "They stopped because they succeeded."

Meera stared at the fractured reflection shimmering in the dim light.

Devendra's words from Rohit's notes echoed in her memory:

"Memory is reflection made permanent."

"He reopened their work," she whispered. "He tried to rebuild what they started. Devendra, Rohit... they were both drawn to the same source. The lineage itself is the link."

Anuj grabbed her arm. "We have to leave. Now. This place isn't safe after dark."

Thunder rumbled again, louder this time, vibrating through the floor. The mirror shimmered once more — faint, breathing.

"All this," Anuj said as they hurried back toward the exit, "everything in these records, every death, every disappearance — it all begins with Devendra."

Meera looked back one last time at the glowing frame.

Her voice was a whisper that trembled with equal parts fear and realization.

"It doesn't just remember," she said. "It waits."

Chapter 5 — The Shadow of Devendra

Timeline: Year 2020 — Three Days After Discovery of the Annex

ORAL HISTORY FLASHBACK: 1940s — The Night of the Storm

The air in the Sub-Level of the British Research Annex still vibrated with a faint, metallic hum. Anuj grabbed Meera's arm, the shared terror between them overpowering any curiosity that might have once driven them deeper.

"The British didn't leave because they failed," Anuj muttered as they scrambled up the stairs. "They left because they succeeded too well. They confirmed the transfer risk. Rohit, Devendra—they're all caught in this... resonance loop."

Meera clutched the fragile British report that confirmed *cross-imprint transfer* and *Source Zero replication.*

"If Devendra figured out the science before they did," she said, breathless, "then he knew how to open the door. But why now? Why is it Rohit being pulled—and who was *Anuja*?"

They emerged from the building as dusk crept over the valley, its violet light stretching long shadows across the grass. The air felt heavier, charged. They had uncovered *how* the pond worked, but not *why* it called. Equations couldn't explain it. The answers, they both knew, were buried in the silence of the village.

The Forgotten Bloodline

Back in the village, they decided their next step was to learn more about Devendra and the family's past. Before they could visit Rohit's father and grandmother, Meera received a call from home.

"I need to go back to Mumbai for a few days," she said reluctantly. "My mother's unwell."

"You go," Anuj replied. "I'll stay. I'll find out more about Devendra—whatever it takes."

She nodded, gave a faint, tired smile, and left the next morning with a promise to stay in touch.

The following day, Anuj made his decision. If the documents and science couldn't explain the mystery, perhaps the old stories could. There were still people in this village who remembered the past—people who spoke in whispers when others mentioned the name *Devendra Thakur*.

He found **Prakash** near the tea stall in the village square, steam curling around his glass as rain began to mist over the rooftops.

"Prakash, I need a favor," Anuj began.

Prakash looked up. "What kind?"

"Have you ever heard of Devendra Thakur? Rohit's great-grandfather?"

The man frowned, searching his memory. “Yes… my grandfather used to talk about the Thakur family. But no one speaks their name now. The new generation doesn’t even know they existed.”

“Could we talk to someone who remembers?” Anuj asked.

Prakash nodded slowly. “My grandmother might. Her memory’s old—but sharper than mine.”

Voices of the Past

Prakash’s grandmother sat on a low cot in a shadowed room. Her eyes were cloudy but alert, her presence commanding even in silence. When she heard the name, her expression shifted.

“What about the Thakur?” she asked, her tone brittle.

Prakash's voice softened. "Dadi, he wants to hear the story you once told us about Devendra Thakur."

The old woman hesitated, fingers tightening around her shawl.

"There isn't much to tell," she said finally. "Thakur is the killer of Somnath's daughter."

Anuj leaned forward. "Who was Somnath's daughter?"

Her voice lowered to a trembling whisper.

"*Anuja*. She was sacrificed near Devta Kund. And then Thakur ran away."

Anuj's stomach tightened. "Sacrificed? Are you sure?"

But the woman turned her face away, muttering, "Don't speak his name. It brings misfortune."

Echoes in Silence

That night, Anuj tried to speak to Rohit's father. The moment he mentioned *Devendra Thakur*, the man's face hardened.

"Don't ask about him again," he snapped, rising abruptly and leaving the room.

Rohit's grandmother was no help either—she stared at the floor, unblinking, as though trapped in a memory she couldn't escape.

For days, Anuj tried again and again. The pattern was the same. Every villager had a version of the story:

Devendra killed Anuja.

Devendra and Anuja were forbidden lovers.

Devendra performed a ritual sacrifice.

None agreed.

But every voice spoke his name with the same shiver of unease.

The Old Man's Truth

At the tea stall the next morning, Anuj and Prakash sat over cups gone cold.

"Is there *anyone* left who knows what really happened?" to *Devendra Thakur* Anuj.

Before Prakash could answer, an old man sitting nearby slammed his glass onto the table. "Who are you to speak that name?" he barked.

Prakash jumped up. "Sorry, Hari Baba, he's not from here."

But the old man's eyes—pale and wet with age—had already changed. Beneath the anger flickered something else: grief, guilt, and memory.

Anuj took a cautious step forward. "Please, I'm only trying to understand. Rohit is missing. His disappearance—Devta Kund—it's all connected to Devendra."

The old man's shoulders sagged.

"You said the Kund?" he rasped. "Then sit down, boy. Because once I tell you, you won't sleep easy again."

Harilal's Story

"Devendra Thakur wasn't like the rest of us," Harilal began, his voice a cracked whisper that carried the weight of years. "He studied the Vedas and mathematics. He said the pond wasn't holy—it was magnetic. That it bent light, reflected *time* itself."

Anuj felt his pulse quicken. “You mean… he experimented on it?”

Harilal nodded slowly. “He believed the water held memory. That if you understood its pattern, you could touch the moment it remembered.”

Anuj frowned. “And that’s why the village suffered?”

The old man’s eyes grew distant. “Because of what came after.”

He took a trembling breath.

“The night everything ended.”

The Night of the Storm

Rain had battered the valley that night—sheets of water tearing branches from trees, lightning shattering the sky.

Devendra's wife had gone into labor with their second child. Lantern in hand, he had rushed into the storm, saying he needed to fetch a doctor from the next village.

He never came back.

That same night, *Anuja* disappeared.

"I saw the pond," Harilal whispered. "It glowed brighter than lightning but made no sound. I called her name—*Anuja!*—but the storm swallowed my voice. When the rain stopped, they were both gone."

Anuj's voice trembled. "Do you believe Devendra killed her?"

Harilal's eyes hardened.

"No. He loved her. Whatever took them wasn't human. Maybe not even of this world."

He turned toward the mist-covered hills.

“Sometimes, on moonlit nights,” he said softly, “people still see them by the pond—hand in hand—their reflections brighter than their bodies.”

The Photograph

Silence fell between them. The air outside was thick with rain again, the kind that didn’t fall—it lingered.

Finally, Harilal reached into his coat and drew out a small cloth bundle. “There’s one more thing,” he said, unwrapping it with care.

Inside was an old black-and-white photograph, its edges curled, its surface faded with time.

“She changed everything for me,” Harilal said softly. “Anuja. I loved her once. But she loved him. She saw his brilliance when the rest of us saw madness.”

He held out the photograph. "Take it. I don't need it anymore."

Anuj accepted it carefully. The paper was cool and fragile. Harilal turned and disappeared into the fog rolling up from the fields.

Under the dim light of the tea stall's flickering bulb, Anuj examined the photograph.

Anuja stood near what looked like Devta Kund, her eyes turned slightly away—as though someone had just called her name. Behind her, almost invisible in the blurred background, a shadow stretched across the water.

Not a reflection.

A figure.

Tall, indistinct, nearly erased by time.

He blinked once.

The shadow did not vanish.

A chill crawled up his spine.

Whether it was a flaw in the old film or something else entirely, Anuj couldn't say.

He slipped the photograph into his pocket, his pulse quickening.

Out beyond the mist, the pond waited.

And he knew now—whatever truth Devendra had touched...

...it had never let go.

Chapter 6 — The Village of Secrets

Timeline: Year 2020 — One Week After the Disappearance

ARCHIVE FLASHBACK: Year 1948 — British Experiment (The Shankh Yantra Test)

The air around the village felt different now—heavier, charged with a strange stillness, as if the entire valley were holding its breath. Ever since Anuj's return, whispers had begun to circle once more.

Villagers spoke of flickering lights near Devta Kund, of faint voices echoing across the hills long after midnight.

Some said it was Devendra Thakur's spirit.

Others swore they'd seen Rohit Sharma standing silently at the pond's edge, his reflection moving before he did.

Anuj wasn't interested in superstition anymore.

He wanted answers—real ones.

Meera Returns

That morning, Meera arrived back from the city. She had tried to lose herself in work, but Mumbai no longer felt real—the sound of traffic, the hum of computers, all felt artificial compared to the call still echoing in her dreams.

When Inspector Karan called to say new evidence had surfaced, she didn't hesitate. Within hours, she was on the first bus winding back toward the mist-soaked valley.

The moment her feet touched the wet ground of the village, the familiar scent of earth and pine gripped her chest.

She met Anuj near the Panchayat road, his eyes weary but alert.

"It's starting again," he said quietly. "People are seeing lights near the pond."

Meera nodded. "Karan told me. There's also a new witness—someone who saw Rohit that night."

Anuj's pulse quickened. "Then we're closer than ever."

Echoes of the Past

Later that day, they went to Rohit's old house. The rooms felt untouched, preserved in dust and silence. Light slanted through the broken blinds in thin golden lines that cut across the furniture like marks of time itself.

Meera brushed her hand along the wall. "It feels like time stopped here."

Anuj set his bag on the table, unfolding Rohit's notebooks and sketches of Devta Kund. Each page carried fragments of obsession—coordinates, equations, drawings of ripples and concentric circles that looked more ritualistic than scientific.

Among the pages lay the faded photograph of Anuja, the woman who had vanished seventy years ago.

Meera studied it closely. "There's something in her eyes," she murmured. "It's like they're reflecting water."

Anuj tilted the photograph toward the light—and for an instant, both saw it: a faint ripple moving across the image, as if something beneath it had stirred.

He inhaled sharply. "Devendra wasn't just a teacher. He was exploring the point where faith and physics meet. The villagers saw the pond as divine—but he studied it. The mountain feeds the pond through a hidden stream. He knew it. Rohit knew it. They were studying the same source."

Meera's voice was almost a whisper. "Then Devendra was the first."

Anuj nodded. "And that's why he vanished."

Rohit's Family History

As dusk deepened, the scent of rain drifted through the air. Meera remembered the conversations she'd once had with Rohit's parents—small fragments that, until now, hadn't seemed important.

Devendra's son—Rohit's grandfather—had been the first to leave the village, determined to escape the rumors and shame.

Years later, Rohit's father had returned, posted there as a government teacher, believing he could rebuild their name in peace.

She remembered his voice, quiet but weighted with something unspoken, when she had once asked about their ancestry over evening tea.

"Rohit's great-grandfather, Devendra Thakur, was a respected teacher," he had said slowly. "One stormy night, he disappeared—and so did Somnath's daughter. People believed they ran away together. Her father was furious. He drove Devendra's wife and child out of the village."

He had paused, his eyes distant with old grief.

"My father changed our surname from Thakur to Sharma. He didn't want the shame to follow us. But my grandmother... she never believed Devendra left willingly. She waited for him her entire life."

In the dim light of the present, Meera's voice trembled. "He never told Rohit."

Anuj closed the notebook. "And now the past has come to find him anyway."

Return to Devta Kund — (Historical Flashback)

It was the monsoon of 1948.

Thunder rumbled like a living thing across the

mountains. The air smelled of metal and rain. Beneath the storm, Devta Kund glowed with an eerie blue phosphorescence that defied nature.

On the rocky bank, a group of British engineers and officers worked under flickering mercury lamps. Their tents and brass instruments looked foreign and fragile against the raw power of the land.

A polished device—a Shankh Yantra of brass and quartz—was being lowered into the pond.

“The quartz beneath the mountain amplifies the field,” one of the engineers murmured. “When the charge aligns with the storm, we should see temporal resonance.”

Major Eddington raised his voice above the rain. “Remember—this is an energy storage test. Nothing more.”

But the sky did not care.

A bolt of lightning struck the tallest pine. The ground shuddered.

The pond's surface began to vibrate, its color deepening from blue to a blinding silver.

A low hum filled the air—then a column of light erupted skyward, twisting, spinning, alive.

The British men stumbled back in terror as the water turned to radiance.

For a brief moment, time itself seemed to bend.

And the pond... remembered.

The Photograph's Secret

That night, in Rohit's old study, Anuj examined the photograph again. As he turned it over, faint letters appeared—glowing softly on the back of the image:

Devta Kund

—followed by the date of Rohit's disappearance.

Meera's voice shook. "It's marking the moment he crossed."

Anuj stared at her. "Crossed into where... or when?"

Thunder rolled again, echoing through the mountains like an answer they weren't ready to hear.

The Final Testimony

The next morning, Inspector Karan arrived with a witness—a shepherd from the northern slopes. His hands trembled as he twisted his cap, eyes darting from one face to another.

"That night," he began, "I saw your friend Rohit. He was at the pond... with a girl. When lightning struck, they both vanished. Just vanished."

Meera leaned forward. "A girl? Do you know who she was?"

He shook his head. "Not from this village. But I would know her face again."

Anuj slid the photograph of Anuja across the table.

The man froze. His pupils dilated, his breath caught.

"This... this is her," he whispered.

Meera's voice broke. "Are you sure?"

"One hundred percent. She was with him."

Silence spread through the room—heavy, immovable.

“Anuja disappeared seventy-five years ago,” Meera whispered.

Outside, thunder cracked across the sky.

Far beyond the window, over the misty hills, a faint blue light flickered once—then vanished.

Anuj pushed back from the table, his voice steady but urgent.

“We have to go back to the pond. Now.”

Meera clutched Rohit’s notebook, her eyes wide with realization.

“The witness said lightning struck when they vanished,” she said. “And Rohit’s equations—they predict it.”

She turned toward the door.

“Rohit didn’t just follow Devendra’s research...”

Her voice dropped to a whisper.

"He was completing it."

CHAPTER 7 — The Crossing

Timeline: Present Day — Year 2020 — Night of the Storm

Location: Devta Kund, Northern Hills

The storm had returned.

Rain lashed across the valley, drumming against rooftops and trees, carrying the scent of wet soil and something sharper – metallic, almost electric. The wind howled like an ancient thing awakened.

In the distance, lightning crawled over the ridge, illuminating the narrow path that led to Devta Kund.

Anuj and Meera walked in silence, flashlights slicing through sheets of rain. The forest was alive with movement — leaves shivering, branches creaking, shadows shifting faster than they could track.

"Are you sure about this?" Anuj asked, raising his voice above the thunder.

Meera didn't look back. Her eyes were fixed ahead. "Rohit's equations predicted a recurrence tonight. The magnetic pulse, the storm, the alignment — everything repeats. If there's a window... this is it."

"Or a trap," Anuj muttered.

She didn't answer.

The Return to the Pond

When they reached the clearing, the rain had slowed to a whisper. The pond shimmered faintly beneath the lightning — no ripples, no disturbance, just an impossible stillness that reflected the storm-torn sky like glass.

Meera stepped closer. Her breath misted in the cold air.

"Look," she whispered.

Anuj followed her gaze. The surface of the water wasn't showing *them* anymore — it was showing **someone else**.

A man stood at the far side of the pond.

Still. Watching.

The rain passed through him like mist.

Anuj's throat tightened. "Rohit...?"

Meera's hand trembled as she lifted Rohit's notebook, its pages fluttering violently in the wind. "He wrote this pattern for a reason."

She turned to the page marked with the lightning symbol and the final equation — the one Rohit had circled three times.

When reflection meets resonance, the boundary dissolves.

Lightning split the sky. The pond flashed blinding blue.

The air vibrated — deep, resonant, alive.

Anuj staggered backward as the compass in his hand spun wildly. Meera dropped to her knees, clutching the notebook as if it were a lifeline.

In the reflection, Rohit lifted his hand.
Slowly. Silently.

And then — so did she.

Her fingertips brushed the water.

The world held its breath.

The Resonance

The blue light surged upward, twisting like a spiral, wrapping around them both. The hum deepened into a low, rhythmic pulse — the same pulse from the sub-level. The one that matched **Devendra's signature frequency** in the old British records.

Anuj shouted her name, but his voice dissolved in the sound.

The pond's surface no longer reflected them; it *absorbed* them. Their shapes fractured into shimmering silhouettes, one overlapping the other — Meera, Rohit, Devendra, and Anuja — faces merging, eyes aligning, time folding in on itself.

For a heartbeat, Meera saw everything.

The storm of 1948.

Devendra reaching toward the light.

Anuja screaming his name.

The British mirror chamber collapsing.

Rohit, standing where she stood now.

Then the vision snapped.

The light imploded inward — a single blinding flash — and silence returned.

The Morning After

When dawn came, the storm had passed. Mist hung low over the forest. The villagers found the clearing deserted.

No footprints. No signs of struggle. Only the faint metallic scent in the air — and the ripples on the pond still spreading outward, though there was no wind.

Inspector Karan stood at the edge of the water, his uniform soaked, his face pale. "No one could survive that storm," he said softly.

But the constable beside him frowned. "Sir... look here."

Half-buried in the mud near the bank lay a notebook, its cover warped, its pages sealed by water.

The last legible line inside read:

'Resonance achieved. Window stable.'

Karan exhaled slowly. "Whose handwriting is that?"

The constable hesitated. "It matches Rohit Sharma's file, sir."

Karan stared at the words. "But that can't be."

He turned the notebook over — and froze.

On the back cover, pressed faintly into the leather, were **two fresh fingerprints**.

Side by side.

One was clearly Meera's.

The other... was not.

Epilogue Moment (Visual Finale)

Far away, deep beneath the hills, a faint hum began again — rhythmic, patient, alive.

In the mirrored dark, two silhouettes stood hand in hand, their reflections slightly delayed, as though time itself were remembering them.

The surface quivered once.

Then the light went out.

End of Season One.

About the Author

Sujeet N. Mishra is an Indian author and storyteller whose writing explores the intersection of mystery, science, and spirituality. His works blend realism with the supernatural, revealing how human emotion, memory, and time weave through unseen dimensions.

Devta Kund: The God's Pond — The Village of Secrets (Season One) is the first instalment in his dark fiction series that bridges myth and modern science, tracing ancestral echoes through generations.

When not writing, Sujeet spends time researching local legends, travelling through remote Indian landscapes, and observing the quiet mysteries of nature — all of which inspire the haunting settings in his stories.

Follow his work and future releases through official book networks and upcoming author platforms.

www.ingramcontent.com/pod-product-compliance
Ingram Content Group UK Ltd.
Pitfield, Milton Keynes, MK11 3LW, UK
UKHW021409190726
13845UKWH00028B/979

9 789334 449976